CLASSIC FAIRY TALES

ILLUSTRATED BY CAROL LAWSON

RETOLD BY HELEN CRESSWELL

PictureLions
An Imprint of HarperCollinsPublishers

For GML

First published in hardback in Great Britain
by HarperCollins Publishers Ltd in 1993
First published in Picture Lions in 1994
10 9 8 7 6 5 4 3 2
Picture Lions is an imprint of the Children's Division,
part of HarperCollins Publishers Ltd,
77-85 Fulham Palace Road, Hammersmith, London W6 8JB
Text copyright © Helen Cresswell 1971
with the exception of *Snow-white and Rose-red*:
Text copyright © Helen Cresswell 1993
Illustrations copyright © Carol Lawson 1993
Licensed by Gresham Licensing Ltd
A CIP catalogue record for this title
is available from the British Library.
The author and illustrator assert the moral right
to be identified as the author and illustrator of the work.

ISBN: 0 00 664 502-X

Printed and bound in Hong Kong
This book is set in 14/19 Goudy

CONTENTS

~ Sleeping Beauty ~

There once lived a king and queen who were married for many years without having any children. Then at last a daughter was born to them, and so delighted were they that they gave a feast for the baby's Christening. Invitations were sent to all the lords and ladies in the land and to far off kings and queens.

Thirteen fairies lived in this kingdom, but the king had only twelve golden plates to set before them, and so he had to leave one of the fairies out.

On the day of the christening the king and his guests feasted merrily, and in the evening before they left, all the fairies presented the Princess with a magic gift. One gave her the gift of wisdom, another the gift of beauty, a third wished her all the riches she desired. And so it went on until the eleventh fairy had spoken, when suddenly the glittering crowd of guests parted and between them went the thirteenth fairy, all in black. She looked neither left nor right and greeted no one. She stopped by the side of the baby's cradle and lifted her arms like great black wings and cried in a terrible voice,

"When the Princess is fifteen years old, she shall prick herself with a spindle and fall down dead!"

Her arms fell and in a great silence she turned and went out of the hall.

Now the twelfth fairy still had not made her gift. It was beyond her power to undo the wicked spell, but she was able to soften it, by saying, "When the Princess pricks herself with a spindle, she shall not die, but fall into a deep sleep lasting for a hundred years."

Even this seemed tragedy enough to the King and Queen, and they gave orders that all the spindles in the land should be burned. As the Princess grew up, growing wiser and lovelier and kinder each day, the fairy's curse began to seem very faint and far away, so that they hardly thought of it at all.

On the Princess's fifteenth birthday a party was held at the Palace. The Princess begged for a game of hide-and-seek. The guests scattered and the Princess herself began to run up and down the stone corridors, looking for a hiding place. At last she came to a crumbling tower that she had never noticed before.

"They will never find me here!" she thought.

She climbed the narrow, winding stairs and came to a studded door with a great rusty key in the lock. The Princess turned it and went inside.

There an old woman sat with a spindle, spinning flax. The Princess stared. All the spindles in the kingdom had disappeared long ago, because of the fairy's curse, and so she had never set eyes on one before.

"Good day, Granny," said the Princess. She had quite forgotten the game of hide-and-seek. "What are you doing?"

"I am spinning," replied the old woman, nodding her head.

"And what is this that whirls round so merrily?" asked the Princess. With these words she took the spindle and tried to spin too.

But she had scarcely touched it before the curse was fulfilled and she pricked her finger with the spindle. She fell back asleep, and the old woman, her work done, went away down the stone stairs with her evil laughter echoing about her.

At the very moment when the Princess fell asleep her guests, too, closed their eyes and slept just where they happened to be – some in cupboards, some behind pillars and others

under the great four poster beds. Even the King and Queen fell asleep in the great hall. Their courtiers yawned and rubbed their eyes and soon were sprawling on the strewn rushes. The horses lay sleeping in the stables, the dogs in the yard, the doves on the roof, the flies on the wall. Even the fire on the hearth stopped its flickering and the meat on the spit stopped crackling. The cook, who was about to box the scullion's ears, began to snore with her arm still raised for the blow. Outside, the wind dropped. Not a bough stirred, not a twig, not a leaf. All slept.

Round the castle a hedge of briers began to grow up, minute by minute. It grew higher and higher, surrounding the whole castle with live green walls of thorn and bramble. Soon nothing could be seen from the outside world, not even a turret, not even a flag on the roof. Within, the clocks ticked to a standstill, the dust settled, there was nothing but sleep and silence.

A legend grew up as years went by about the sleeping Brier Rose, as the Princess was called. Princes came from far off lands to try to force their way through the high thickets. But the greedy thorns clutched them like hands so that they could never escape and were left there to die.

Then, one day, when the hundred years were nearly up, a bold and handsome prince rode by. He met an old man working in the woods, who told him the legend of the beautiful sleeping Princess. He begged the Prince not to try to enter, and warned him of the terrible fate that had befallen the rest.

"I am not afraid," replied the Prince. "I am determined to go and see Brier Rose with my own eyes."

He rode to the thicket, never knowing that this very day the one hundred years were ended, and the Princess would wake from her spellbound sleep. As the Prince drew near, he saw to his astonishment that the hedge was covered with large and beautiful flowers. They seemed to be unfurling their petals even as he watched. As he rode up, the briers curled back and made way for him so that he could pass unharmed, and then closed up again into a hedge behind him.

In the courtyard he found brindled dogs lying asleep, nose on paws. He saw doves on the roof, heads under wings. He pushed the door and entered the silent palace and saw there the King and Queen themselves, lying by the throne. The Prince had to step over the sleeping forms of guards and courtiers and passed next through the kitchen where the cook had stood for a hundred years with her arm raised ready to box the scullion's ears. Nearby sat a maid who had been fixed in time while she plucked the black feathers from a fowl on her knee.

The Prince went tiptoe through the palace, and so great was the hush that he could hear his own breathing. Then at last he came to the chamber where Brier Rose lay sleeping.

The Princess looked so beautiful lying there that the Prince knelt by the bedside and kissed her gently on the lips.

"Nobody seems to want it, and it seems a pity to waste it."

She sat on the biggest chair, but it was too big. She tried Mother Bear's chair, but that was still too big. Then she sat on the wee small chair and crash, the leg broke and the chair and Goldilocks went tumbling to the floor.

"O dear!" said Goldilocks. But she was still determined to try the porridge, so she went all round the table, tasting from each bowl.

First she tried the bowl belonging to the Great Rough Bear – because that one was the biggest. It was too hot. So was the porridge in Mother Bear's bowl, but when she came to the last one, belonging to the Wee Small Bear, it was just right, and she ate it all up. She had not *meant* to eat it all, but it was so delicious that she went on tasting and tasting till it had all gone.

"I'm tired now after my long walk," said Goldilocks. "I must find somewhere to rest."

She went upstairs and lay on the bed belonging to the Great Rough Bear, but it was too big, and she couldn't settle. Then she tried Mother Bear's bed, but that wasn't right either. But when she lay on the Wee Small Bear's bed it felt exactly right, and she was so comfortable that soon she was fast asleep.

Not long after, the three bears came home from their walk.

"Someone's been sitting in my chair," growled the Great Rough Bear in his great rough voice.

"Someone's been sitting in my chair, too," said Mother Bear in her soft mother voice.

"Someone's been sitting in my chair and broken it all to pieces!" cried the Wee Small Bear in his small shrill voice.

"Someone's been tasting my porridge," growled the Great Rough Bear in his great rough voice.

"Someone's been tasting my porridge, too," said the Mother Bear in her soft mother voice.

"Someone has been tasting my porridge and has tasted it all up!" cried the Wee Small Bear in his shrill small voice.

Then the bears went upstairs.

"Someone has been lying in my bed," growled the Great Rough Bear in his great rough voice.

"Someone has been lying in my bed, too," said the Mother Bear in her soft mother voice.

"Someone has been lying in my bed and here she is!" cried the Wee Small Bear in his shrill small voice.

Just then Goldilocks awoke. She saw the big furry faces of the three bears looking down at her, and with a loud shriek jumped up and rushed down the stairs and out of the cottage with her hair flying out behind her.

"She is afraid of us!" laughed the Great Rough Bear in his great rough way.

"She is afraid of us!" laughed the Mother Bear in her soft mother way.

"She is afraid of us!" laughed the Wee Small Bear in his wee shrill way.

As for Goldilocks, she didn't stop to draw breath till she was safely home again. And she never again went into a house when she found the door standing open, because for all she knew those three bears might have gobbled her up. How was she to know that they only liked porridge and wild honey?

~ Cinderella ~

There was once a man whose first wife had died, and so he married again. He did not pick so well the second time. His new wife was spiteful and bad-tempered and to make matters worse, she had two daughters who both took after her.

This man already had a daughter, and she was kind and gentle and beautiful. So the stepmother and her daughters were thoroughly jealous of her, and soon set about making her life as miserable as they could.

They gave her all the dirty work in the house. She scrubbed and scoured and dusted all day long while her new sisters lay polishing their nails or prinking themselves in the glass. They wore jewels and silks and satins while their poor sister had only a few rags to her back. They slept on soft feather mattresses, deep and warm, while she shivered on straw in the draughty attic.

And she patiently worked and shivered and half-starved without saying a single word of complaint to her father.

At the end of the day when all the work was done, she would sit huddled among the cinders in the chimney corner of the kitchen, trying to keep warm. Even this did not make the ugly sisters sorry. Instead, they laughed, and gave her the nickname of Cinderella.

One day, the king of all the land gave a great ball for his son, the prince. The stepmother and her daughters were invited, and were soon busily planning what they would wear and how they would dress their hair.

While the two ugly sisters posed before the glasses, trying out sashes and twirling their hair into ringlets, Cinderella was sent rushing hither and thither to fetch and carry, to sew and press, so that everything would be ready on the night of the ball. Instead of being grateful for her help, the two sisters mocked her.

"How would you like to go to the ball, Cinderella?" they asked.

"Oh, I would!" she cried wistfully. "But people would only laugh. Look at me, in my old rags!"

"Laugh? I should think they would!" cried the two sisters. "A fine sight *you* would be at the King's ball!"

On the great day Cinderella worked harder than ever in her life before, trying to send her sisters off to the ball looking their very best. And when the last bow was tied and the last ringlet curled, they *did* look their very best – though even that was not saying very much.

Off they went with a proud flurry of rustling skirts, out to the waiting coach, with not so much as a wave of the hand to Cinderella, let alone a thank you. When the sound of the carriage wheels had died away and she was alone at last in the great, empty house, Cinderella crept back to her usual place by the hearth, and began to cry.

After a while she heard a knocking at the door, and drying her eyes, went to answer. In stepped a little old woman who looked like a beggar in her tattered cloak.

"Why are you crying, child?" asked she.

"Because… because…" Cinderella did not like to say why she was crying.

"You need not tell me," said the old lady surprisingly. "I know quite well why you are crying. It is because you want to go to the ball."

Cinderella stared at her.

"I am your godmother," explained the other then. "Your fairy godmother. And now,

child, there's work to be done. Go out into the garden and fetch a
pumpkin, quick!"

Cinderella was out in the garden searching for a pumpkin before she
had even time to think. When she brought it back, her godmother rapped
it smartly with a long black stick – or was it a wand? – and there in a trice stood a golden
carriage! It winked and glittered and shone bright as the sun itself.

"Two mice!" ordered the godmother, without a blink.

Cinderella opened the pantry door and as two mice came scampering out – poof! A wave
of the magic wand and they were high-stepping horses with flowing manes and rearing
heads.

"What about a coachman?" murmured the godmother. "Run and fetch the rat-trap, will
you?"

Cinderella did not wait to be asked twice. Off she ran to fetch it, and next minute there
stood a stout coachman with brass buttons and a large three-cornered hat.

"If you look behind the watering-can beside the well," went on the godmother, without
so much as the twitch of an eyebrow, "you will find six lizards. We could do with them, I
think."

Sure enough, there were six lizards exactly where she had said, and a flick of that busy
wand transformed them instantly into six tall footmen with dashing liveries.

"Well!" exclaimed the fairy godmother then. "That carriage could take a *queen* to the
ball. Do you like it?"

"Oh, it's beautiful!" cried Cinderella. "But Godmother, I still can't go to the ball!"

"And why not?"

"My dress! Look at me! Whoever saw a sight like this at a king's ball?"

"That is easy enough," replied the old lady. "Stand still a moment, child, and shut your
eyes."

Cinderella stood quite still, her eyes tight shut. There was a slow, cool rustling, a breath of scented air and a soft silken brushing and then "Open!" commanded that thin, high voice.

Cinderella opened her eyes.

"Oh!" she gasped. It was all she could say. "Oh!"

About her billowed the most beautiful dress she had ever seen, sky blue and stitched with pearls, threaded with silver. And there, beneath the hem of her skirt, glittered a pair of shining crystal shoes.

"Glass slippers!" gasped Cinderella.

"Off you go now, child," said her godmother briskly. "Off to the ball and enjoy yourself!"

Cinderella gathered up her shimmering skirts and stepped into the golden coach. The footmen bowed. The coachman lifted his whip.

"Wait!" cried the godmother.

Cinderella put her head out of the carriage window.

"Home by twelve sharp! Do you hear? Not a minute later!"

"I shall be back," promised Cinderella.

"Listen for the clock," warned her godmother. "Not a single moment after the last stroke of twelve. If you're even a second late —"

"What?" cried Cinderella in alarm. "What will happen, Godmother?"

The old lady waved her arms.

"Poof! Gone! Coach to pumpkin, horses to mice, coachman to rat – poof! Gone! Gone! All of it!"

"I'll remember," cried Cinderella. "I promise. The last stroke of twelve! Goodbye, Godmother! And thank you!"

She had a last glimpse of her godmother's shabby figure and then the coach was rolling on its way. She, Cinderella, was off to a king's ball!

When at last the golden coach reached the palace gates the news was quickly spread about that a great lady, certainly a princess, had arrived at the gates. Servants and flunkeys ran to bow and open doors and make a way for Cinderella through the crowds of staring guests. For she was so beautiful that all the people stood quite still to watch her as she passed, and even the music faded as the fiddlers laid down their bows in wonder.

The king's son himself watched her walk among the whispering guests. He went to greet her, and was in love before he had even reached her side. He led her on to the floor to dance and the fiddlers picked up their bows again and began to play.

All the evening long the two of them danced together. The prince could not bear to leave Cinderella's side for even a moment. The other guests were filled with envy and curiosity, and the two ugly sisters were angriest of all. Not a single dance had either of them had with the prince all night.

"Whoever can she be?" they cried, craning to peer at her each time she whirled by. Not for a single minute did they suspect that the beautiful stranger was none other than their sister, Cinderella.

Cinderella herself was so happy that she forgot all about the time. The great ballroom clock was already beginning to chime the hour for midnight when she suddenly remembered her godmother's warning and her own promise to be home by twelve.

"Oh!" she cried. "I'm late! The time!"

Before the astonished prince could collect his wits she had darted off and was out of the ballroom and running down the great marble staircase to her waiting coach.

Six… seven… eight… the bell was chiming.

The coach clattered away out of the palace courtyard. At the top of the staircase the prince stood looking left and right for a sign of his vanished partner. He set the servants to search and they ran all through the palace, but in vain. She had gone. Only there, lying half way down the stairs, was a tiny glass slipper – Cinderella's. Sadly the prince picked it up and wandered away. He did not dance again that night.

Meanwhile, Cinderella was hardly out of the palace gates when – poof! The spell was broken. All in a moment she found herself out on the empty road and of the shining coach, the footman and the coachman, there was not a trace. From the corner of her eye she saw, running over the road, a thin dark shape that might have been a lizard. And that was all. Clutching her thin rags about her she set off home. Safely there, she climbed up to her cold attic and fell asleep, dreaming of the ball and the handsome prince.

The prince himself did not sleep at all that night. He paced up and down his room, clasping the glass slipper.

"I must find her," he said out loud. "And when I have found her, I shall marry her, and make her my princess."

Next day the prince called the Royal Herald.

"Come with me," he commanded. "We will search the length and breadth of the kingdom to find the young lady whose foot this slipper fits. For she is the one I will marry."

Soon the news was spread about the town and the king's herald was going from door to door reading his proclamation and trying the slipper on one foot after another. He had not known there were so many feet in the world. Then at last he and the prince came to the house where the two ugly sisters had been eagerly awaiting his visit, their hair tightly curled and their legs trembling with excitement. One of them, for sure, would fit her foot into the glass slipper and become the prince's bride.

At last they heard a loud knocking on the door, and the notes of the herald's trumpet.

"Quick!" hissed their mother. "Sit down and look as if you weren't expecting him. And make sure one of you gets that slipper on!"

With that, she sent a servant to open the door, and next minute they were all curtseying

to the king's messenger.

The two ugly sisters tried with all their might and main to fit their great feet into that dainty slipper. They squeezed and tugged and twisted and muttered and groaned, but all in vain. At last, sulky and red-faced, they gave up the attempt, trying hard not to catch their mother's eye.

"Is there no other young lady in the house?" asked the herald then. "I have orders to miss not a single one, whoever she is."

"No!" cried the three ladies together. "There's no one else!"

But it was too late. The herald had already opened the door of the kitchen, and saw Cinderella sitting there. He bowed politely and offered her the slipper. She held out her foot – and it slid in smoothly.

"It fits!" cried the ugly sisters together. "It can't! It's a trick!"

Cinderella smiled, and taking from her pocket the other slipper, placed it on her other foot. And at that moment, her fairy godmother appeared and with a touch of her magic wand transformed Cinderella's rags into a snow-white bridal gown.

Only then did the prince recognize her as the beautiful stranger at the ball. The ugly sisters and their mother hurried off, afraid of what might happen to them when their wickedness was discovered.

But Cinderella forgave them willingly, and was driven off with her prince in the king's own coach. And they were married that very same day, and lived happily ever after.

~ The Frog Prince ~

One evening a young princess went into a wood and sat down under a lime tree by a spring of clear water. She had taken her favourite plaything with her, a beautiful golden ball, and kept tossing it idly into the air and catching it again.

Each time she threw it higher and higher, until at last she threw it too high and too far, and missed catching it as it fell. It began to roll away from her, away and away, and before she could run after it, rolled right into the spring itself.

"My ball! O, my ball!" cried the Princess in dismay.

She went and leaned right over the edge of the well, but the water was very deep and she knew that she could never reach to the bottom of it. She began to cry, because she had really loved her golden ball, and could not bear to think that she would never play with it again.

"I loved it best of everything in the whole world," she sobbed. "And I'd give anything – everything I've got, to have it back again. All my jewels, all my fine clothes – everything!"

As she finished speaking a frog suddenly put its flat green head out of the water and asked, "Princess, why do you weep so bitterly?"

"O frog, I have lost my golden ball!" she cried. "It has fallen into the well and now I shall never see it again!"

"You *may* see it again," replied the frog, "if you let me help you. I heard what you said

just now. I do not want your jewels or your fine clothes. But if you will love me, and let me live with you, and eat from your little golden plate and sleep upon your bed, then I will bring you back your ball again."

He sat with his green head cocked and looked at the Princess with his great round eyes, and she looked back at him.

"What nonsense he talks!" thought the Princess. "How could he possibly climb out of the well? And as for coming to live with me at the palace – it's impossible! But he may be able to dive down and fetch my pretty ball, so I'll pretend to promise what he asks."

"Very well, frog," she said out loud. "I will agree to what you ask. And now – dive and fetch me my ball quickly – do!"

So the frog splashed down into the water and disappeared. Next minute he came up again with the ball in his mouth.

"O thank you!" cried the Princess, overjoyed. "My ball – my beautiful ball!"

She picked it up and ran gaily off towards the palace, quite forgetting the frog and her own promise.

"Princess, wait!" called the frog after her. "Remember what you promised!"

But the Princess kept on running, and soon was safely home, her adventure forgotten.

Next day, the Princess was just sitting down to her dinner when there came a strange, soft pattering noise as if slippered feet were coming up the marble staircase. Sure enough, next moment there came a gentle knocking at the door, and a voice said:

"Open the door, my Princess dear,
Open the door to thy true love here!
Remember the words the two of us said
By the fountain cool in the greenwood shade!"

The Princess ran to the door and opened it, and there stood the frog, whom she had quite forgotten! The sight of him frightened her so much that she slammed the door shut again in his face and hurried back to her seat. The King himself was sitting at the table.

"Who was that at the door?" he said.

"Only a nasty frog," replied the Princess. "My golden ball fell into the well yesterday, and he fetched it out for me. But he made me make a silly promise, to let him come here and live with me, and now he's wanting to be let in!"

As she was speaking the frog was knocking at the door again, and saying his sad song:

"Open the door, my Princess dear,
Open the door to thy true love here!
Remember the words the two of us said
By the fountain cool in the greenwood shade!"

"You must let him in," said the King. "If you made a promise, you must keep it. Open the door."

Much against her will the Princess went and opened the door, and the frog came hopping in and went right over to the table.

"I am hungry," he said to the Princess. "Pray lift me on to a chair, so that I may sit by you."

She did as he asked, though she could hardly bear to touch him, and when she herself had sat down again, he said, "Push your plate a little closer to me, so that I may eat out of it."

The Princess was forced to obey, though she did not at all like the idea of sharing her plate with a frog.

When he had eaten as much as he could, the frog said, "Now I am tired. Pray carry me upstairs and put me on your own little bed."

The Princess was bound by her promise to do as he asked. She picked up the frog very gingerly, between her fingers, carried him upstairs, and with a shudder dropped him on to her own bed. He crept up on to the pillow, and there he slept all night long. But when morning came, he jumped up and hopped down the stairs and out of the palace.

"Thank heaven!" cried the Princess. "Now he has gone, and I shall see no more of him!"

But she was mistaken. That night as she sat at table there came again that same soft slippery footstep on the stair, and that same gentle knocking at the door. Once again the Princess was forced to feed the frog from her own golden plate, and take him up to her own bed to sleep.

On the third night, when again the frog visited her, the Princess began to regret her promise bitterly.

But on the third morning when she woke, it was to find the frog gone already from her pillow. And there, standing at the foot of the bed, was the most handsome prince she had ever seen, gazing at her with eyes that were loving and gentle and strangely like those of the little frog.

"Dear Princess!" cried the Prince then. "You have broken the spell at last!"

He told her how he had been enchanted by a wicked fairy. She had changed him into a frog, and told him that he would never again take human shape unless he could find a Princess who would take him from the spring and bring him home with her, to feed from her own plate and sleep upon her bed.

"And now you have done this," cried the Prince, "and I love you dearly, and want you to come with me to my own kingdom and marry me, and be my queen."

And so it happened. Next day the Princess drove off with her Prince in a fine golden coach drawn by six white horses, bound for his own kingdom, where they married and lived happily ever after.

~ Rapunzel ~

A man and his wife both longed to have a child. As years went by and still there was no sign of one, they began to despair. But one day the wife was down by the stream washing clothes when a frog put his head out of the water and told her that soon her wish was to be granted.

The wife was overjoyed, and hurried home to tell her husband, who immediately set about making a wooden cradle ready for the baby.

Now next to the cottage where these two lived was a great, overgrown garden, which belonged to a strange old woman whom they had hardly ever seen. People said she was a witch, and were afraid of her.

One day the wife was peering over the wall into this garden when she saw a clump of green rampion growing there. Immediately she began to long for a taste of it, though she had never been particularly fond of it before.

"Dear husband, I must eat some rampion or die!" she told him when he came home from working in the forest. "Climb over the wall and fetch me some, I beg you."

The husband did not like the idea at all.

"It doesn't belong to us," he told her. "And as for that old woman who owns the garden, for all we know she may be a witch, and if she catches me out – what then?"

"What nonsense!" cried the wife. "Witch indeed! I must have some rampion, I tell you, or I shall die!"

And so the man, although he knew full well that the old woman *was* a witch, waited until twilight and then climbed softly over the wall and began to pull up the rampion as quickly as he could. But when he straightened up to climb back over the wall, he found himself face to face with the old witch herself, eyes a-glitter in the gloom.

"How *dare* you climb into my garden and tear up my plants!" she cried in a terrible voice. "I have caught you red-handed, and now it will be the worse for you!"

The poor man, shaking and trembling, explained how greatly his wife had longed for the rampion, and begged the witch to forgive him.

"Never!" she cried. "But I will make a bargain with you. Your wife is about to have a child. I will let you go free and take with you as much rampion as you like, on the condition that when the child is born *I* shall have it, to bring up as my own."

The man agreed, for he was so terrified that he hardly knew what he was saying, and scrambled safely back over the wall with the stolen rampion and a heavy heart.

Soon afterwards, a daughter was born, and when she was only a few days old the witch came and carried the child off with her. She gave her the name Rapunzel (which is another name for rampion).

When Rapunzel was twelve years old the witch locked her in a tall stone tower that stood in the thickest and darkest part of a great wood. It had neither staircase nor doors, only a little window in Rapunzel's own room right at the very top.

Whenever the witch wanted to enter, she would stand below and call up, "Rapunzel, Rapunzel, let down your hair!"

Rapunzel had long yellow hair, which she wore in plaits wound about her head.

When she knocked at the door, a hoarse voice called out, "Lift the latch, and the door will open. Come right in, my dear!"

Little Red Riding Hood lifted the latch and went in. She saw her Grandmother lying in bed wearing a big frilled nightcap and with the blankets pulled up to her chin.

"I'm sorry to find you in bed, Grandmother," said she. "I've brought you some cakes that Mother has baked, and a pat of butter and some new laid eggs. And here are some flowers I picked myself to cheer you up and make your room look bright."

The Wolf (for the Wolf it was, under the frilled lace nightcap) told her to put the food in the pantry and to arrange the flowers in a vase.

"Now you must come and lie beside me and rest," he said, when Red Riding Hood had finished.

She went up close to the bed, and thought how strangely her Grandmother had changed now that she was sick.

"O Grandmother, what great ears you have!" she said.

"All the better to hear you with, my dear," said the Wolf.

"O Grandmother, what great eyes you have," said Little Red Riding Hood.

"All the better to see you with, my dear," replied the Wolf.

"O Grandmother, what great arms you have," cried Red Riding Hood.

"All the better to hug you with, my dear," said the Wolf, and he stretched them out towards her, but Red Riding Hood stepped quickly back and gasped,

"O Grandmother, what great *teeth* you have!"

"The better to eat you with!" cried the Wolf then, and he sprang up from the bed to devour her. But just then a wasp flew through the open window and stung him on the nose. The Wolf let out a great yowl, and as he howled the door opened and an arrow flew straight in and pierced the wicked Wolf through and through.

Little Red Riding Hood turned and saw, standing in the doorway with his bow in hand, the Green Archer, who was keeper of the forest for the King.

"I saw you talking with the wicked Wolf, little maid," he said, "and came to save you. Your Grandmother is safe and sound at my house. It was Puck the fairy who changed himself into the wasp and made the Wolf howl as a signal for me to shoot my arrow. For I don't like little girls to be eaten up, even when they do disobey their mothers and wander away from the path and speak with wolves."

Little Red Riding Hood's face turned so red that it almost matched her cloak.

"I shall never do it again," she promised. And she never did.

Snow White
~and the~
Seven Dwarfs

A queen sat sewing by the window one day when the snow was falling. She lifted her head to see a raven walking on the white lawns, and as she did so, pricked her finger. A drop of blood fell, and in that moment the Queen made a wish.

"I wish that I might have a little daughter, and that her skin might be as white as snow, her lips red as blood and her hair black as a raven's wing." She spoke the wish out loud and when she had finished the raven spread his black wings and flew off into the swirling snow.

Not long afterwards a daughter was born to the King and Queen, and the Queen, remembering her wish, called the child Snow White. And as she grew older her skin was white as snow, her lips were red as blood and her hair shone like a raven's wing.

After a few years the Queen died and the King married again. His new wife was beautiful and proud. She would gaze and gaze at herself in the magic glass that hung in her room, and say to it,

"Mirror, Mirror on the wall,
Who is the fairest of us all?"

Then the glass would answer,

*"Pale as the moon, bright as a star,
Thou art the fairest, Queen, by far!"*

And the Queen would smile at her reflection in the cold glass and stretch her neck like a swan and preen.

But Snow White grew more and more beautiful each day, and when she was seven years old she was even fairer than the Queen herself.

The magic mirror could not tell a lie, and so when next the Queen asked it,

*"Mirror, Mirror on the wall,
Who is the fairest of us all?"*

the reply came,

*"Fair as the day, O Queen, you are,
But Snow White is lovelier by far!"*

At this the Queen turned white with rage. She sent for a huntsman and told him to take Snow White deep into the forest and there to kill her. But when the huntsman drew his knife to plunge it into her heart, and Snow White began to cry and beg for her life, he remembered his own children at home, and slowly let the knife fall.

"Run as far off as you can," he told her. "If ever you return, we shall both lose our lives."

Then he turned and left her, and on his way back to the palace he killed a fawn and cut out its heart to take back to the Queen, pretending it was Snow White's.

Now Snow White was alone in the dim green forest and as she ran the brambles clutched at her dress like live hands and the sharp stones cut into her feet. But the wild animals that roamed by let her pass without harming her, and she ran and ran all day until it was evening. Then, in the dusk, she came upon a little house, the first she had seen all day, and because she was so tired, went inside to rest. Inside, everything was very small and yet neat and clean as could be. There was a small table set out with a white cloth and seven little plates and seven little loaves and seven little glasses with wine in them. By the wall were seven little beds, neatly made with not a wrinkle in the counterpanes.

Snow White was so hungry that she went right round the table taking a little nibble of each loaf, a forkful of vegetables from each plate and a sip of wine from each glass.

Then, because she was so tired after her day in the forest, she went to the row of beds and tried first one and then another till she found the most comfortable. She lay down and went straight to sleep.

Soon afterwards, the owners of the house came home. They were seven dwarfs, who worked all day deep in the mountainside with pick and shovel, digging for gold and precious stones. In they came and took off their boots and left them in a row by the door. Then they lit the lamps and saw at once that things were not as they had left them.

"Who has been sitting in my chair?" said the first.

"Who has been using my fork?" said the second.

"Who has been nibbling my bread?" said the third.

"Who has been picking at my vegetables?" said the fourth.

"Who has been drinking out of my glass?" said the fifth.

"Who has been cutting with my knife?" said the sixth.

"And who has been eating off my plate?" said the seventh.

Then one of them went over to his bed and saw a dent in the counterpane and he cried, "Someone has been sitting on my bed!"

Then all the rest ran up to their beds crying, "And mine! And mine!" until the seventh dwarf went to *his* bed and found Snow White herself, fast asleep.

"Sssssh!" he hissed loudly to the others. "Sssh! Come and look!"

All seven dwarfs crowded round the bed whispering and nudging one another and all fixing their eyes on Snow White's beautiful face.

"What a lovely child!" they whispered. "We mustn't wake her!"

So all through the night the seven dwarfs took turns to watch by Snow White's bedside, an hour each until morning came. When she awoke and saw the seven dwarfs Snow White was frightened and covered her eyes. But they spoke gently to her and asked her name and how she had come there alone through the thick forest. Snow White told them her story, and when she had finished the first dwarf asked,

"Can you cook and sew and spin? Can you dust and sweep and kindle fires? Can you knit and bake and can you trim a lamp?"

Snow White could do all these things, because her stepmother had kept her hard at work at home. And so the dwarfs said that she could stay with them and look after the house while they went off each day to dig for gold and silver in the mountains.

Each day, before they set off in the grey dawn the dwarfs would warn Snow White,

"Take care to let no one in. One day the Queen will find out where you are and try to harm you."

All this time the Queen had thought Snow White was dead, and was so sure that she was now the most beautiful in the land that she had not troubled to use her magic glass. But one day, when she had nothing else to do, she went and sat before it, smiled at her reflection and asked,

> "Mirror, Mirror on the wall,
> Who is the fairest of us all?"

And the glass answered,

"Queen, thou art fairest here, I hold,
But in the forest and over fell
Snow White with the seven dwarfs doth dwell
And she is fairer, a thousandfold!"

At this the Queen was mad with hate and envy, and lifted her arm to shatter the mirror into a thousand pieces. But her arm fell, and she thought, "No. It is not the mirror I must destroy, but Snow White!"

Next day she stained her face brown and dressed in rags like a pedlar woman and set off into the forest to the cottage of the seven dwarfs. There she stood beneath the window with her big hat shading her face and called out, "Wares to sell! Wares to sell!"

Snow White put her head out of the window. "Good day," she said. "What have you to sell?"

"Pretty trinkets," replied the wicked Queen. "And coloured laces for your waist!"

She held up one of plaited scarlet silk, dangling it under Snow White's eyes so that she thought, "Surely I may let this pedlar in? She seems kind and honest, and has such pretty things!"

She opened the door and the Queen went in.

"Gracious, child!" she cried. "How badly your dress is laced! Here let *me* do it, with this pretty scarlet lace, and you shall have it for a penny!"

Snow White stood quite still while the pedlar threaded the new red lace with nimble fingers. But the wicked Queen pulled the laces tighter and tighter and tighter till at last all the breath was squeezed out of Snow White's body and she fell to the floor and lay there as if she were dead.

"That's the end of *you* and your beauty!" cried the spiteful Queen, and hastened back towards the palace.

When the dwarfs came back and found Snow White lying lifeless on the floor they guessed at once what had happened. One of them seized a knife and cut the scarlet lace and at once Snow White drew in a great sigh and began to breathe again. The dwarfs gave a shout of joy, and next day when they set off in the mists for the mountains they begged her to take care, and be on the watch for the wicked Queen.

That very morning the Queen herself rose early and went to the magic mirror.

"Mirror, Mirror on the wall,
Who is the fairest of us all?"

When the mirror gave the same answer as before the Queen could not speak for anger. In terrible silence she dressed in a disguise, a different one, and took up a tray of bright combs and painted one of them with deadly poison. She set off to the dwarfs' house and there she knocked on the door and cried, "Fine wares to sell! Fine wares to sell!"

Again Snow White looked through the window, and said, "I cannot open the door – I dare not! I have promised to let no one in!"

"There is no need to open the door," replied the Queen. "Just look at my beautiful combs. See, I will pass one up for you to try."

She picked out a carved comb of finest ivory. Snow White took it from her and put it into her hair and no sooner had she done so than she fell to the floor in a deadly swoon.

"There you may lie!" cried the wicked Queen, and went her way.

Luckily, that day the dwarfs came home from the mountains early and found Snow White before she was quite dead. They gently took the poisoned comb from her hair and after a time she opened her eyes and sat up. When she told them what had happened they warned her yet again to beware, and again Snow White promised that she would.

That very night the Queen went to her magic mirror again. When she received the same reply as before and knew that Snow White must still be living she shivered and shook from head to foot with rage. She pointed her long white finger into the mirror and it pointed back at her.

"Snow White shall die!" she cried. "Even if it cost *my* life!"

All night long she secretly worked at a poisoned apple. One side of it was rosy and shining, the other clear and green. Whoever took a bite from the red side was sure to die.

At dawn the Queen went gliding out to the woods dressed as a peasant's wife. When she came to the dwarfs' house she knocked and Snow White put her head out of the window.

"I cannot open the door," she said. "The dwarfs have made me promise not to."

"Very well," said the old woman. "It doesn't matter to me whether you do or not. But perhaps you'd like this pretty apple as a present before I go?"

Snow White shook her head.

"What is the matter?" asked the peasant woman. "Do you think that it is poisoned? Silly girl – see, watch me!"

She turned the green side of the apple to her lips and bit into it.

"There!" said she. "If it were poisoned, do you think *I* should have eaten it? Here, take the rest and eat it!"

Snow White longed for the shining red apple with its juicy flesh. She took it from the old woman, bit into the rosy skin and next minute fell to the ground.

"This time nothing shall save her!" cried the Queen, and hastened back to the castle. There she went and stood before the magic mirror and at last it gave her the answer she wanted, *"Thou art the fairest, Queen, by far!"*

When the dwarfs came home, laden with gold in the twilight, they found Snow White lying there and lifted her up and splashed her face with cold water and did everything they could think of to bring her back to life. It was in vain. Snow White's eyelids never flickered, not the faintest breath floated from her lips. For seven days and seven nights

they watched by her side, but there was not the least stir of life. For all that, Snow White was still so beautiful that they could hardly bring themselves to believe that she was really dead.

"We can't bury her in the cold ground!" they cried. And they made a coffin of glass and placed her in it and wrote her name on it in gold letters. They carried the coffin to the hillside and one of the dwarfs always sat by it and watched, day and night. And all the birds of the air came singly out of the sky to lament the death of Snow White, the owl, the raven and at last the dove.

Snow White lay many years on the bare mountainside and still she seemed only to sleep. Her lips were red as blood, her skin was white as snow and her hair black as a raven's wing just as they had been in life.

It happened one day that the son of a king came riding by and saw Snow White within her glass walls. He read the gold lettering and learned her name, and that she was the daughter of a king.

"Give her to me!" he begged the dwarfs. But they all shook their heads and refused to let her go.

"I will give you gold and treasure," pleaded the Prince.

Again they refused. "We will not give her up for all the treasure in the world!"

"Then I shall stay here on the mountain all my days looking on Snow White," said the Prince. "I cannot live without her."

At this, the dwarfs pitied him and could not deny him what he asked. They themselves helped to lift the coffin, and as they did so, the piece of poisoned apple fell from Snow White's lips. She opened her eyes, lifted her head, and cried in astonishment, "What's happening?"

The Prince, overjoyed, lifted her from the coffin and told her the story of how she had been poisoned by the wicked Queen and had lain like one dead for more than seven years.

"But now you have come to life again," he said. "And I love you better than all the world. Come with me to my father's kingdom and marry me!"

And so Snow White said farewell to the seven dwarfs and went with the Prince to his father's castle where a great feast was prepared for their wedding.

Among the guests invited was Snow White's wicked stepmother. She dressed herself in her finest clothes and when she was ready, stood before the magic glass and smiled proudly.

"Mirror, Mirror on the wall,
Who is the fairest of us all?"

Then the glass replied,

"Fair as the day, O Queen you are,
But the new bride is lovelier, by far!"

At this the Queen's fury was so great that she lifted her jewelled hand and struck the glass and it broke into a thousand pieces. Then she went out and rode to the wedding, so that she could see with her own eyes this bride who was even more beautiful than herself.

And when she went into the hall and saw that the bride was none other than Snow White, she flew into such a passion of hate and envy that her heart burst and she fell down dead.

But Snow White and the Prince were married that day and lived and reigned happily ever after.